Urban Psalms

Of Recovery and Grace

Theresa John

FIRST EDITION

ISBN: 978-1-7393670-3-9 (paperback)

Urban Psalms is published by TC Publishing

For information, please direct emails to: info@ibelieveican.co.uk

TC PUBLISHING

Dedication

I would like to dedicate this book to Jesus, my Lord, my Saviour, and my best friend. Without Him, this book would never have been possible. He is my hope and my everything. Secondly, to my three amazing children, Katie, Kaine, and Jordan. I pray they will be encouraged and inspired to dream big and believe that they can achieve their dreams with determination and hope for the future. And last but not least, to my mum, Denise, for never giving up and holding on to hope in all circumstances.

Table of Contents

Praise for Urban Psalms

I'm privileged to have Theresa as a friend. She has real experience of overcoming some dark areas in life, and her writing draws from that wealth of knowledge. As you read this book, you'll have the opportunity to connect with the truth carried in her words, a truth that can literally transform your reality.

Paul Lloyd
Author, International Speaker and Leader
Senior Pastor- Victory Outreach Manchester
Regional Pastor UK/Germany Region

What a privilege to endorse Theresa John's book 'Urban Psalms.' I've had the privilege of walking alongside Theresa through many years of her journey, and seeing her transformation first hand has been very special to me. She is very special to me. Her creative writing gift, both through spoken and written word, is beautiful, unique, and like the strokes of brushes on a canvas, painting pictures with her words. I am proud to know her and to have her as our assistant, but most importantly, our friend. Experience who she is through her book! You won't be disappointed!"

Vicky Lloyd
Author, International Speaker and Leader
Senior Pastor's Wife- Victory Outreach Manchester
Regional UK/Germany Region

Introduction

Language and words have always been something that fascinates me. The importance of communication, how we construct sentences, the tone of our voices, the use of punctuation in the written word all captures my attention.

Writing has been instrumental in my life's journey. From a young age, I would write, whether short stories, attempts at songwriting, or poems that helped me process emotions. I love that words can help to move, inspire, communicate deep truths, and have the ability to instil joy and laughter. We hold a great responsibility with our communication. The power of life and death are in the tongue (Proverbs 18:21); what we speak holds weight. Those who have a word gift have an opportunity to leave a mark on this world, for good or for bad. How we use that opportunity is up to us!

This book of poems came from my deep love of my Lord Jesus Christ, the Word (logos) Himself. It came from deep emotion, journeying through addiction, sickness, and many of life's ups and downs. My desire is that this book would help the reader find and experience hope. As our world gets ever darker, there is a light of hope; the word of truth and the love of a heavenly Father is available to all, and it is my hope that you will see that we can experience every emotion and still have the anchor of hope for our souls as we navigate the storms of life.

Because of the Word of God, I am 10 years free of addiction and walking in my purpose. Journey with me through the Urban Psalms, a group of poems laced with personal experience and God-inspired scripture.

Words

In the beginning was the Word, and the Word was with
God, and the Word was God…

Words are powerful; words are divine.
Words can make someone smile and make that same
person frown.

Creativity, a pen in the hand or the tongue in your mouth,
constructing carefully selected sentences,
each word placed together like foundational bricks
building a pattern.

Cementing and solidifying truth or lies.
Words hold the ability to deconstruct a soul with a
throwaway remark
… in the next breath, such joy to see the restoring of a
heart.

The restoring of a heart with words as sweet as honey,
kind to the soul.
Words that embrace, sympathise, console.

The power of life and death is in the tongue, power that
is in our control.

How do you wield the sword of flesh that rests in your
mouth?

They say, "Don't trust your tongue when your heart is
bitter."

Venom that spews from infected wounds; the enemy
dresses words like a skilled counterfeiter.

The same tongue that blesses also curses.

The perception of deception, counterfeit claims of love
spring forth from words of hate.

So, we pray, for the words we speak hold weight.

In the beginning, was the Word...
Place a guard upon my mouth lest I sin in what I say.

I desire words that bring life, not those that can cause pain.

When the winds of adversity arise, and the waves crash all around.

The temptation to speak from discouragement can be the loudest sound…

…Peace… Be still!

The power of life and death is in your tongue.
Speak to the wind.
Speak to the waves.

Rise up, oh sleeper, get up from the grave!

Sharper than a double-edged sword is the Word we have, the Word of truth that cuts and prunes and separates with great grace.
Let the Word of God embrace you, change you, and transform you.

In the beginning, was the Word, and the Word was with God, and the Word was God…

…Meditate on His character; think on who He is.

You were created like Him, your image forged as His.

Allow the meditations of your heart to bring forth pleasing words from your lips.

Not bitterness or resentment that throw words so heavy they sink ships.
Not the waves of adversity, rather the washing of His Word.

Spring up, oh well, sing with a heart of thanksgiving!

The Word of God breathes life, abundant life, the only life worth living.

Open Doors

I believed I couldn't…
So, I didn't.
Scared and fearful,
years of disappointment left me tearful.
I was cast out, abused, and rejected.
Lost, abandoned, and quite frankly disrespected.
Looking for a way out.
Or a way in?
My troubles had me all boxed in.
I was looking for a key to fit the door,
But not one would fit…
A bit like me.
I never really fit.
I tried fitting in with all the wrong people;
I never found the right groove.
Looked for acceptance from men and kept coming up
empty.

I was being cut and shaped by every disappointment.
Moulded and burnt by every hurtful word.
Although life got painful and led me to drugs and to crime.
I'm so grateful that the cry of my heart was heard.
You see, something within began to rise up.
The spirit of survival, a new way to fight.
My past began to fade, and from it, I took flight.
Left the past as my past and began rewriting my end.
Walking a different way and setting a new trend.
It looked like rejection, lies, drugs, and pain.
Were writing me off so my life would fade away.
But the shaping and cutting, the burning and moulding.
Were just what was needed to find that right groove.
I stepped out from the darkness; I opened my eyes.
The clouds parted, and all of a sudden, I could see.
Everything I had been through, every twist and turn.
It wasn't just for my journey; I had now become a key!
Every lesson I have learnt is a key to be used.
For men and for women, for young and old.
To break through barriers and to open doors…

Addiction

Crying shame, where's the shoulder?
Heavy weight upon my back;
people wonder why I turned to smack.
I want oblivion, pure and clear;
get out my works and cook my gear.
I know it's wrong, can't make it right.
But I will get clean; it's a long, old fight.
Running nose, streaming eyes,
cramps, sneezes, and nasty lies.
It will ravage your body and steal your soul when
getting clean is your only goal.

It can be done; it's been done before.
Become the Christian and not the whore.

I took liberties; it was plain to see,
But I know there's potential inside of me.
Please, God above, I trust You're there;
awaken me to love and care.
Love for You and others too;
love for myself created by You.

The Journey

On a journey, but only my King knows where.
Appointed and anointed to spread love and to care.
Back in the day, someone planted a seed;
they saw deep within that I had a great need.
When I believed I had no one, feeling lost and rejected,
they told me a story that I have slowly respected.
They spoke of a man who was sent from above.
He was sentenced to death to reconnect God's first love.
Now to the beginning, while I was still blind,
at the enemy's table, I frequently dined.
Hurting and lost, I thought I'd never be found,
the enemy's lies had me so tightly bound.
The banquet he gave seemed so tasty and free.
When I felt so alone, he said, "Come with me."
I didn't know why, but it didn't feel right;
his grip had a hold so wrong but so tight.
I ventured down a dark road that I slowly despised
as he fed me his poison of crack-coated lies.
I got so far in the darkness, l had lost my way.
Struggling to fight and get through each day.
Now the devil was laughing, had my life in his hands.
But the Man up above had, for me, other plans.
I started fighting the darkness to find a new way.

But due to drugs, crime, and madness, I would have to
pay.
I stood in the dock and said, "Guilty's my plea."
Some time behind bars, after which I'll be free.
I acted like a big woman with nothing to fear.
But someone was watching and saw every tear.
The time had now come; my heart was prepared
to find out the truth so readily shared.
I thought I'd had troubles and had carried a weight,
but my weakness and sorrows had someone else in a
state.
A man had been beaten so I could be whole.
Despised, whipped, and pierced, He's the Saviour of
souls.
God sent His own son so that we can be saved.
A pathway to Heaven Jesus has paved.
He did no wrong and lived a sinless life,
but for our transgressions, He paid the ultimate price.
He intercedes for rebels, for you and for me;
When we accept Him as Lord from our sins, we are
freed.
Now, knowing all this, I went back to my ends.
I got back on the gear and tried to witness to friends.
But that wasn't His plan; that plan was by me
because I couldn't believe what I just couldn't see.
His mercy and grace, which cannot be earned,
saw the enemy's tactics dramatically turned.
The work that He started, He is following through.

I pray that He keeps me strengthened and true.
I couldn't do it in London, felt lost and alone.
Yet, moving to Salford felt strangely at home.
I've wholly surrendered my life to God's hand.
Got my Bible and read; on His Word, I now stand.
I'm not going to lie; it's a battle we are in.
But Jesus is Champion, so with Him, we will win.
I used to fight in the world with bottles and knives.
Now God's given a new armour against the enemy's lies.
I have a shield of the faith and sword of the spirit,
I'll continue to fight because I'm in it to win it.
God has always been faithful; He loved me first.
Fighting for me when I was at my worst.
The devil comes only to kill, steal, and destroy.
A life in Christ brings the ultimate joy.
I am a new creation and dead to sin,
God is taking me places that I couldn't imagine.
Sin has no control, for I've been set free.
Christ in me is the hope of glory.
He is my Lord, my Saviour, my mighty King.
I must fight for souls, and to Him I will bring
the ones just like me, who are hurting and lost.
Fighting the devil, whatever the cost.
He thought it was over, that the battle was done.
But with Jesus is Lord, which means we overcome.

Surrender

Been used and abused by women and men.
Beaten up and battered, again and again.
Always in pain, alone and afraid,
selling my body just to get paid.
I thought I was lost, that I'd never be found
until I was dead, buried under the ground.
You see, trust was an issue, I have to admit.
So, who other than God to lift me out of the pit?
It's a journey I'm on to seek His great light;
to move forward in Christ with spiritual sight.
I pray He would grow me with passion and fire.
I will fight in the spirit because the devil's a liar.
I can't be held back because my past is over.
I don't have a lucky charm or some four-leaf clover.
I have Jesus as Lord; He paid the ultimate price,

healing my life from every hurt, pain, and vice.
What has been done for me, He has done for you, too.
So, if you want to know more, here's what to do:
Surrender your heart, relinquish your will,
get on your knees, be quiet, be still.
Let Him know that you want Him, you need Him today.
It's free; Jesus has done it. Your debt has been paid.
Ask Him into your life, wherever you're from.
He will help carry your burdens, for our Lord is so strong.
He will always be there. He is waiting on you.
Take a step of faith; what is there to lose?

Marks and Scars

If you look closely, you'll see scars on a battle-worn face.
The marks and scars on my face tell a story.
But the marks and scars on the inside run deeper.
Some scars self-inflicted, others inflicted upon me.
Even though the marks on my face are visible, I can choose not to see them,
avoiding them in mirrors and veering away from photos.
But…
the inner wounds are ever visible,
the mark of domestic violence runs deep;
cuts and bruises disappear, scars begin to fade,
internal triggers of control spark unhealthy behaviour rooted in pain,
shuddering in fear at the mention of your name…
Wondering what is wrong.
Expecting the worst at every turn.

Treading on eggshells, trying not to crack;
being awakened, patterns of behaviour become clear,
patterns that have identified who I am…
Shame creeps in…
I thought I was healed?
The closer I get to Jesus, the more my broken heart is revealed.
There is beauty in the brokenness.
As everything inside feels overlooked, disregarded, and rejected
God begins to rebuild…
putting me back together
piece by piece.
Filling my brokenness with gold.
The marks and scars testify to His goodness.
The marks and scars become His story.
The marks and scars bear witness to the saving grace of Christ.

Hidden Cries

Tied up, stuck in a rut,
I was offered a way out, but always a "but."
I thought I knew it all, but knew nothing at all.
Never needed any help 'cause I had no goals.
Aiming for nothing so I'd nothing to lose.
Death or life put before me; what would I choose?
My mind was set; I was good for nothing.
Saw potential in others, but what could I bring?
I had glimmers of hope, but they were stolen away.
My dreams were crushed. I had nothing to say.
I could blame the enemy, but I silenced myself.
Jealousy and comparison began to damage my health.
An emotional wreck. I was wild and unstable.
I sat myself down at the enemy's table.
I made myself comfortable, feet up, leaning back.
Slowly but surely, I got addicted to crack.
It messed with my head, but I wouldn't let on.
Pride covered it up and tried to show I was strong.
Behind closed doors, it was a different story.

Crying out for help, I just wanted to break free.
Who was I calling on?
Was anyone there?
Lost, damaged, so broken, but did anyone care?
I wasn't too sure, but I had nothing to lose.
Death or life? Now what should I choose?
I could feel something changing, something deep down inside.
I began to feel peace, no longer wanting to hide.
My heart had been opened, ready to hear,
about a man they call Jesus who could calm every fear.
Jesus, they told me, knew all I had done.
They said He was calling, asking me to come.
He really was calling, asking to follow His ways.
They said He'd forgive me and that my debt had been paid.
True to His word, Jesus has set me free.
I've submitted to Him, and my enemies flee.
I now have a purpose. God has the plan.
He is the King of kings, the Great I Am.
My trust is in Him, forever on the throne
He advances me forward, for He is God alone.

Who am I?

(Adaptation of Psalm 8, from the Holy Bible)

When I think about the wonders, the works of Your hands,
I sit, and I ponder…
Who am I?
I lift my eyes to the hills, Your majestic works.
I look to the skies, the canvas of the heavens,
And I wonder…
Who am I?
Through praises and the melodies of Your children. You build a wall around my enemies.
You show your care to me.

But why?
Who am I?
Who are we?
What is mankind? What are human beings that You care for us?
Who are we?
We are the work of Your hands,
And You are the Lord our God.
The One who created the angels, crowning them with glory and honour…
Who are we?
You seat us in heavenly places and call us Your own…
Who are we?
We are carefully crafted by Your loving hands; we are shaped and moulded,
Your children, your workmanship…
Who are we?
We are the wayward prodigals who walked away,
wandering in the wilderness, disconnected from our Father…
Who are we?
We are created beings, created by the Creator.
We are a little lower than the angels and given life through Christ.

What is mankind? Human beings that You care for us?
When we were disconnected. You sent Your only son as a sacrifice.
Lost in our sin-filled wanderings,
Jesus paid the price.
Who am I?
Who are You?
Who are we?
We are Yours.
You are God, our God,
Lord of lords and King of kings,
Majesty, Saviour, Healer, and Redeemer.
We are redeemed.
We are renewed.
We are desired.
We are valued.
We are precious in Your sight.
Who are we?
We are the Lord's, His sons and His daughters.
We are worth dying for.
He calls us loved,
He calls us His own…
Lord, our Lord, His name is majestic in all the earth
…and He is ours.

The Attraction of Melancholy

Have you ever felt sad for no apparent reason?
A conundrum of the mind.
External things have no impact.
Internally foggy with a mild chance of rain.
Raining from the inside out,
The healing waters flow,
Washing down flushed cheeks.
The cool liquid lingers over warm skin.
There is almost a refreshing in the sadness,
The melancholic moments,
The pause in between
…

Like bridges on a country road,
slowing down to breathe,
you recognise the road less travelled
and realise you have travelled here before.
The beauty in the valleys,
The dew drops settled on intricately veined leaves.
The attraction of melancholy,
Seeing in a way that only sadness helps you see.
You have come this far.
And whilst weariness looms,
Your eyes widen, brighten even.
The tears of your melancholy watering the garden of
your dreams.
Noticing that not everything is as it seems.

Shadow

No matter where I go,
I can't escape my shadow.
That shaded part of me.
The one hidden in the dark.
Light creates shadows yet banishes the dark.
A shadow of my former self creeping up behind me.
Then disappears.
...
I know she's there.
...
Embrace me in Your love,
Envelop me in Your light.
You, oh Lord,
Your Word,
The lamp for my soul,
The light for my path.
...

Shine!
Banish the darkness,
Eradicate the shadows,
the darkness that covers truth.
...
Arise, oh God.
Scatter the enemy.
Arise and let the light of Your glory
SHINE!

Depression

Chains, bars, and prison walls,
Locked in the mystery of the mind,
Like a large steel door closing ever tighter,
the key turns loudly, committing your thoughts to a life sentence.
The darkest night seems to grow ever darker,
Like a rain cloud in the midnight hour
Without a flash of lightning to brighten the skies.
Hopelessness envelopes you,
Wrapping you in a disappointing blanket of every failure and mistake you've ever made.
Depression…
pressing, suffocating, and inoculating any joy you may have had.
Laughing is a distant memory,
The sound of which becomes unfamiliar,
even painful to the ear.
Other people's happiness only amplifies the dark echoes in your soul.

Cries of the heart reach up to the highest heavens…
"Weeping may endure for a night, but joy comes in the morning."
The Lord is close to the broken-hearted;
A broken and contrite spirit He will not despise.
His truth comforts and embraces.
His truth exposes every lie.
Hope against hope.
…
The cracking begins as the shell starts to break.
New life springs forth!
Oh, weeping may endure for a night,
But joy comes in the morning!
Every failure becomes a lesson and not the final say.
The light begins to break as dawn is on its way.
Shifting shadows give way to glimmers of hope
as the sun begins to rise.
Weeping endures, but only for a night.
Morning is here, My child.
…
Open your eyes!

Why Suffering? Why Not?

Pain, hurt, brokenness, and lies.
Depression brings compression to the mind and eyes.
Blinded in darkness, searching for a light
at the end of yourself where strength is not might.
Crying out for an answer every night and day;
Why, oh God, would you leave me this way?
Oh, mighty God, Creator and Healer,
You make declarations,
But believe no one can hear you.
A rollercoaster of emotions, rising, falling,
doing loops and spins, feeling sick and dizzy.
Shame, condemnation, lies and deceit.
The stories in the mind keeping you busy.
Busy giving in to despair,
leaning back into hopelessness…
If your God is so good, why are you suffering?
God of miracles, is He?
The barrage of conflict is often puzzling,
But on reading His truth, an awakening begins.

See, there's no promise to be without trial or affliction.
The opposite is true when you fully dive in.
To be a true disciple will actually cause friction.
There's a burden we must carry in walking with Christ.
See, the name of Jesus cannot be thrown around in vain.
He carried His cross for the salvation of all.
Whipped and beaten in continual pain,
on His heart the whole time were our names.
Our Saviour and Lover,
Our very best Friend,
Through pain and suffering brought captivity to an end.
To represent Christ, we must carry our own cross.
We can help bear each other's burdens,
but our loads are our own.
See, Christ humbled Himself to that death on the cross,
and now intercedes for us at the right hand of the
throne.
So, count it all joy, my brothers and sisters.
For each trial brings about a great opportunity,
To build perseverance, faith, and endurance,
To build up each other in Christ's own community.

Roots

Searching, reaching, drawing…
A never-ending intricate network of inter-twining
woven roots,
Like the searching of our souls
…
All things were founded by Him and for Him.
In Him, we find peace.
In Him, there is fullness of joy.
In Him is where we find our rest.
Draw near to Him, and He will draw near to you.
Like the system of roots buried beneath the earth,
they push their way desperately through soil and grit.
Searching, reaching for life-giving water.
Growing down deeper and deeper,
Burrowing into His love, His truth, His embrace.
Searching, reaching, drawing.
Drawing from the well of living water.

Spring up! Burst forth!
Remain ever rooted, ever grounded,
Built up in the love of Christ.
Like mighty oak trees bearing fruit in spring.
Growing deeper in the winter,
Searching, reaching, drawing, forever rooted in Him.

Hold on to Hope

Uncertainty, unknown and unclear,
But, in the midst of it all… Hope.
Physical isolation, social solidarity,
But, in the midst of it all… Hope.
Storms, chaos, unspoken fear,
In the midst of it all… Hope.
Against all hope, hope and believe.
Believe in the certainty of salvation.
Hope in the coming of our Lord Jesus Christ.
Know that He is the same yesterday, today and forever.
Be clear that without faith, it is impossible to please God.
And in the midst of it all… Hope.
He is the One who stills the storm.
He spoke creation out of chaos.
His perfect love casts out all fear.
In the midst of it all… Hope.
Hold on to your hope and stand steadfast,
Knowing that the battle belongs to the Lord.
And in the midst of it all… Hope.
For those who hope in the Lord will never be put to shame.

Joy

Joy is a choice that comes from the inner being.
If the joy of the Lord is strength,
Why do I feel so weak?
But,
Wait…
His joy,
Not mine.
His joy is not something to be mustered up alone.
Joy comes from Him alone.
My body is the temple of His Holy Spirit,
A carrier of His presence.
Therefore, joy comes from within.
Though sometimes buried beneath the cares of this
world.
The truth declares it is there.

Making a Stand

The hate, the names, the shame
Spitting venom, taking lives.
Hate breeding hate and unjust scales
When silence screams like a child in the dead of night.
Riots and screams are drowned out by unspoken words.
Ignorance, belligerence, silence, and violence.
This isn't a one-time reaction.
Years of injustice, compressed and condensed, brought to a point of implosion.
The inner work of oppression, case upon case, resulting in an outpoured explosion.
Hate does not drive out hate.
Pain misinterpreted, confusion, angst, and discouragement.
Step up, speak out,
Do not stay silent; stand.
Silence says so much more than the ignorance you try to hide when you bury your head in the sand.

Educate yourself.
Though it costs you all you have, get understanding.
Compassion is love in action.
Understanding every person's value created in God's
image.
No division, no dissension,
United in Christ, we make our ascension.
We stand together.
Communities and cultures so different,
Yet so able to unite in diversity.
Created in the image of God above.
Celebrating our differences.
Marvelling in the similarities with love.
A husband
a wife
a mother
a father
A son
a daughter
Called and chosen. A royal priesthood.
The enemy comes to steal, kill, and destroy.
To steal your identity. Destroy who you are.

Life, and life in abundance, is given to all.
No discrimination. No separation.
Only separated to Him.
We pray, we unite, we stand.
When we have done all to stand, we stand.
We stand for equality. We stand for justice.
We stand for mercy. We stand for love.
Humankind; He has told us what is good
and what it is the Lord requires of us:
to act justly,
to love faithfulness,
and to walk humbly with your God.

Speak

My words paint a picture; let me tell you a story.
From rags to riches,
From darkness to light of glory.
There's a song that says,
"You've got the words to change a nation, but you're biting your tongue, spent a lifetime stuck in silence, afraid you'll say something wrong."
See, there's a wealth of wisdom to be mined.
Words that are chain-breakers,
Words that breathe life and build city-takers.
But... here we are,
Bound down, cast out...
It's not over.
Intimidation, fear, doubt creeping in,
Questioning what's been hidden inside of you.
See, I wish I could take you to a place where my mind takes me every day.
It's like a magical mystery tour;
Long, winding roads and deep rabbit holes,
Bright, luminous colours but a somewhat colourless soul.
Beyond the fear, the darkness, the silence, there is an open space.
Like a bright green meadow on a warm spring day.

Spinning in circles, wandering through daisy-covered grass.
Wondering... will this spacious place ever last?
Struggling to speak, not wanting to communicate fear.
Why is it so hard to trust?... Keep quiet; no one will hear!
Lift your head, keep moving, even a crawl.
Try not to trip up. Try not to fall.
My child,
What kept you so quiet? Who silenced your voice?
I gave you that voice; what you speak is by choice.
You hear the laughter, feel the hurt and the pain,
But you must remember it was I who called you by name.
I gave you the words; they are not yours but are Mine.
Don't put on that mask and say that it's fine.
What's been hidden inside will rise up to the surface.
When I bring the release, there is not one who'll reverse it.
I have given you faith. I've given My Word.
I have given promises, and yet there's still more to learn.
Don't hold back, don't hide, don't fight it, just stand.
Use the Word, keep moving. I've given you the land.
See, I'm not just Your Saviour; I'm not just your Lord.
I'm your Father, your Teacher, your Lover and Friend.
I'm the One who wrote your whole story from beginning to end.
Father, is that You? Jesus, do You hear me?

How did You hear the words I never said?
Were You there in the darkness? Was it by You I've been led?
I don't understand. I know what I'm like.
Why would You give me promises and bring me into Your light?
My child, you are special, like all My creations.
Hand-picked, shaped, and moulded by My loving hands.
My child, you are not alone; there are many others inheriting this land.
Dominion is yours, and My kingdom is unshakable.
I choose you because of your weakness because it is I who is able.
Now the words that I have given you, they are not for your fame.
The words hold power to bring glory to My name.
The great I Am, the Way-maker, Chain-breaker.
I bring beauty from ashes, Saviour of souls.
Where once there was darkness, I made pathways of gold.
I love with a perfect love, which casts out all fear.
Now speak out those words so My people may hear.
I'm raising up warriors from the least and the last.
Releasing my destiny and erasing their past.

What If?

What if we stopped for a moment?
What if we looked beyond ourselves?
What if we all played our part?
With a world spun out in chaos, death and darkness looming over nations.
What if, instead of fear, we respond with faith?
What if, instead of anger, we breathe peace?
What if, instead of isolation, we stood together?
What if we look beyond the now?

We have been slowed from the everyday commotion of motion.
Be still and know that I am God.
What if God allowed us to be shaken?
What if, on the other side, is a great revival?
What if this moment is not just a moment, but setting the stage for a great harvest?
Limits have been removed. The people of God exercise their voice – what if?
What if God's poets arise with hope-filled words, speaking truth and life?
What if songwriters and musicians penned songs of deliverance?
What if God is creating creativity inside you right now?

The church goes beyond a building and is not the walls,
the pews, and the pulpit.
The church is God's people.
What if?
What if you were created for such a time as this?
What if your prayers hold much more weight than your
presence?
What if we humble ourselves and pray and seek God's
face?
Where, oh Death, is your victory?
Where, oh Death, is your sting?
What if?
What if it is your turn to prophesy?
What if it's now to speak life?
What if God is waiting to activate your words?
In death, breathe life.
In despair, speak hope.
In darkness, shine bright.
Created in the image of God.
A carrier of light.

Enmeshment

Broken love and broken lives
Broken minds and broken lines
Crossing borders
Breaking boundaries of the soul
Picking up the pieces
And trying to rebuild that vacant hole
Mismatched fragments
In a life less ordinary
Shards of brokenness
Enmeshed together
Exhausting emotional intelligence
Undrawn lines
Mark a recipe for disaster
Cooking up co-dependence
Temperature set to boiling point
Feelings running over
Spilling out
No self-control…
Entangled…
Awakened
You start to unravel
The only one who feeds your soul
The daily bread by which we live
The one true dependence

Dependency will set you free
But not on her or him or them
But on the One
The One who truly gave it all
The only One who can truly fill that vacant hole
The lion of the tribe of Judah
Roaring for your soul
Chasing down the predators
Rewriting history like an editor
Clean slate
Go again
Leaning into Christ alone
The foundation and the cornerstone

Mindfield

There is a battle raging in the mind.
Which side are you on?
Dark versus light,
Lies against truth,
The battle is in your mind, and the prize is your soul.
The heaviness of darkness,
Clouds that colour your judgement
Distorting the very truth that sets you free…
Whispers of doubt, feeling lost and confused,
Walking through the mindfield of the mind…
CRASH… Another hit, another lie.
Failure, never good enough,
Worthless, give up…
Flight or fight?
Darkness can surely be overwhelming.
The lies dressed up so well they look like truth
and so easily tripped over.
…

You shall know the truth, and the truth will set you free.
Fight, not flight!
The battle isn't easy;
The battle can be drawn out…
But, my friend, the battle is already won.
You see, Jesus is the light of the world.
In Him, darkness cannot abide.
Light does not even carry a shadow,
Yet we have been called to carry His presence.
We are His temple,
His royal people.
Therefore, the light of Christ must surely dwell within us.
The truth, the Gospel; we fight with His word and His name
We fight, we stand, we live.
You will have troubles, my friend,
But,
Take heart, for the Lord overcame them all.

You Are Mine

My Father in Heaven,
Are you the one who chose my name?
How did you form me in my mother's womb and
entrust me to this uncertain land?
Was abandonment a part of your plan?

When you lured me into the wilderness,
A barren place where you took me by the hand,
My feeble arms and weakened knees,
You strengthened me to stand.

My Father in Heaven,
Hallowed in all the earth.
It is only by Your Word and love
That my life was fully birthed.
Why, with such love, would you allow
Seemingly endless rejections.
Countless years wandering in the desert.
Allowing time for such painful reflections?
Was rejection simply redirection?

In a world that promotes satisfaction in anything other than you.
Fatherless nations crying out for attention.
Groaning earnestly, inner longings held with conflicting tension.
The ease of the fast with the pain of the wait.
When instant gratification outweighs the journey of pursuit.
The road I took became a shaded route...
...
I am the Light of the world, says the Lord.
How have you become entrenched in offence?
My timing is perfect, my promises are true.
Yet unbelief and distrust seem to have darkened you.
I am the same yesterday, today and forever.
My Word will not return void.
Wait on Me, My child, be patient and true.
I am in the waiting, right in the middle
I am there. I haven't forsaken you.
Though your pain is raw, the feelings are real.
I am great and mighty, holy and true.

I am above all things, above your circumstance and way
above what you feel or the things you do.
Your heart has become hardened, and you feel there's no
way back.
Buy don't forget who I am.
I created your heart. I named you. I know what you
need.
Return to Me, My child, the Lord, your Shepherd, for
in Me there is no lack.
You have been waiting on Me, but My child.
I am waiting on you.
I haven't moved. I am still here.
Step in, make a decision. It will be different this time.
Let's walk together, for I am yours, and you are Mine.

Prince of Peace

Struggling to breathe…
Like a blow to the stomach.
Winded.
Emptied.
A deficit.
A gaping hole.
A space that only You can fill.
Disassociated.
Numb.
A whirlwind of uncommunicated emotions.
Stillness.
Stuck.
Unable to move.
Watching the world keep turning.
Disconnected from the dam built up inside.
A wall.
Holding back the rush of tears.
They threaten to break forth.
Flooding my soul.
My chest tightens.

Grief gripping my inner being.
A shadow of what could have been.
Attempts to darken.
The light of what is…
Inadequacy, opinions, lies.
Creeping thoughts of the past.
Try to suffocate the life of the present….
Remember me, oh Lord.
Remember me in the light of Your unfailing love.
I run to You.
Like a weaned child to its mother.
You alone calm and quiet my soul.
Running to the River of Life.
I thirst.
I drink.
You fill.
That vacant space overflows.
Entering in Your sanctuary.
The light of Your glory.
My distorted perspective vanishes.

Thanksgiving.
Praise.
The refreshing of Your presence.
My safe space.
Uncommunicated emotions.
Fully understood.
Abba Father.
The One who knows my heart.
Lead me through the mysteries.
As I wait on You.
My Prince of peace.

This is the Space

This is the space
Unoccupied.
Vacancy available.
A room in my heart.
Many have rented here before.
Walking through with dirty shoes.
This is the space.
A room in my heart.
Yet not to rent but to own
deep cleaned.
Purified.
Sanctified.
A space once tainted.
Men who claimed squatters rights.
Long since evicted.
This is the space.
The space where my Saviour dines.
A space to eat in the presence of my enemies.
This is a house called home.
A place that Jesus owns.

I Didn't Know I Died

I didn't know I died.
I missed the memo I was drowning.
As the waves swept over my head.
The weight of the tide pulled me under.
I thought I was going with the flow.
Turns out i'd been swept away.
As the water flooded my lungs.
I sunk into a docile state.
Living in a dream.
Numb yet aware.
Aware but not alive.
I didn't know I died.
Until I started to breathe again.

Voices

Tumultuous sound waves.
Noise upon noise.
Unending tides.
Sweeping back and forth.
A world that never stops talking .
Layers of sound.
As every decibel amalgamates.
One loud noise.
A constant hum of opinions.
Everyone has a platform .
Yet no one really has a voice of their own.
Regurgitated false information.
Every singer a new song writer.
Dancers tiktoking their time away.
Influencers swept away by ever changing waves of
human opinion.
Its all just noise.
Unless its anchored by the truth .
Everything goes quiet when we seek His voice.

Feeling inspired?
Why not create your own Urban Psalm

Feeling inspired?
Why not create your own Urban Psalm

Feeling inspired?
Why not create your own Urban Psalm

Feeling inspired?
Why not create your own Urban Psalm

Feeling inspired?
Why not create your own Urban Psalm

Feeling inspired?
Why not create your own Urban Psalm

Feeling inspired?
Why not create your own Urban Psalm

About the author

Theresa started writing at a young age. She has a passion for navigating life with creativity at the helm. In 2013, as a struggling drug addict, Theresa had an encounter with Jesus, and there began a beautiful transformation process. Similar to a butterfly, this transformation came with a cocoon, hiddenness, and lots of goo! But with this debut book, Theresa enjoys 10 years set free from a life of crime and addiction, with a desire to reach others with the gift of creative writing. Now, she is spreading her wings and sharing her writings for all to see.

For speaking engagements,
please contact Theresa at:
urbanpsalms1@gmail.com

Review Ask

Thank you for reading this book. If you found this book useful, please consider leaving a short review on Amazon to help other readers know what the book is about and how it can help them.

Printed in Great Britain
by Amazon

46156282R00046